For Momo

FIRST PUBLISHED 2003 BY WALKER BOOKS LTD

87 VAUXHALL WALK, LONDON SE11 5HJ

10 9 8 7 6 5 4 3 2 1

© 2003 Bruce Ingman

THIS BOOK HAS BEEN TYPESET IN FUTURA BOOK

PRINTED IN ITALY

British Library Cataloguing in Publication Data:
a catalogue record for this book is available from the British Library

ISBN 0-7445-5553-1

TERMS AND CONDITIONS FOR READING THIS BOOK!

1. When you get to the end, say "Again, please".
2. Put book under the bed or somewhere safe.
3. No sticky fingers or ripping pages.
4. Lots of giggling.
5. Say please.
6. Look smart.
7. Say thank you!

Amelia
David
Daniel

Hannah
Jane

Boston
← 5521 km

Liz
Patrick

Sydney
↓ a long wa

Photographs:

Toy Story (p 22) – Walt Disney Co.

King Kong (p 22) – RKO courtesy of The Kobal Collection

Star Wars (p 23) – Lucasfilm Ltd courtesy of The Kobal Collection

Thanks to Jessica Ingman, Cait Robertson and Ellie Robertson

BAD NEWS I'M IN CHARGE!

WALKER BOOKS
AND SUBSIDIARIES
LONDON • BOSTON • SYDNEY

Bruce Ingman

My mum used to say, Danny,

Tidy up!

Tuck your shirt in!

OUTSIDE NOW!

And take that **THING** with you.

That **THING** was my

antastic superdoopa metal detector.

... 25 bottle tops ... 3 spoons ... a tin trumpet ... potato smasher

I found all sorts   of things...

ettle ... screwdriver ... a dog collar with "Reginald" on it ...

The finder of this charter is the new owner and ruler of this land. By law.

I didn't waste any time ...

to be some **chang s** around **h re!**

I appointed my
TOP GANG.

I gave them identity cards and the secret password to get them entry to Top Gang HQ for secret meetings.

I set about ruling

my land.

List of Changes

1. Stay up late

2. Chips with everything

3. Treats all the time

4. Every Wednesday teachers to wear funny hats

5. Wild parties every week

6. Wear what you like

7. Make your mum + dad wait outside in the car while you visit the toyshop for hours & hours

8. Friends around every day

9. No dentists! No hairdressers!

10. ~~All~~ Pets in school

11. Mum + Dad in bed by 8 o'clock

IT'S OFFICIAL!

School

was so much more fun.

straight to my room.

My new rules were very popular.

But sometimes I had to put my

foot down...

Lights Out!

HOW TO EMBARRASS YOUR KIDS!

Monday

Judge cabbage competition.

Tuesday

Open garden fête.

Wednesday

Launch ship.

Thursday

Judge beauty contest.

Friday

Open toothbrush factory.

Saturday

Attend opera concert.

Sunday

Open another garden fête.

Monday

Then one day an unexpected visitor from

CENTRAL
OFFICE

came looking for me. There was more to being in charge than I thought.

Wednesday
Launch ship.

Thursday
Judge beaut...
contest.

I couldn't take another
week of this!

with all the ministers →

and gave each one ←

Minister of Being Polite

Minister of Shaking Hands

Minister of Transport

Minister of Tidying Up

Minister of Rainy Days

But I kept the best one for myself:

S PROUDLY

MINISTER of FUN!